아이들은
놀라워라

Children
are
amazing

박노해 사진에세이 05

아이들은 놀라워라
Children
are
amazing

PARK NOHAE PHOTO ESSAY 05

느린걸음

아이들은 놀라워라
가장 먼저 울고 가장 먼저 웃고
자신들의 새로운 길을 향해
거침없이 나아가는 아이들은,
아이들은 놀라워라

Children are amazing.
Children, who cry first, laugh first,
find their own new way and
move ahead without hesitation,
children are amazing.

CONTENTS

Preface · 13

Photography

A boy setting off on a journey · 18 Children baking potatoes · 22
A handsome young farmer · 24 Rice threshing day · 26 Beyond that mountain · 28
Boys in the Hebron wilderness · 32 Carrying her little brother on her back · 34
A child tending seeds · 36 Fishermen's family at Branta harbor · 38
Brothers taking a bath · 40 Carrying buckets · 44 Time to bake roti · 46
In a toddy palm grove · 48 Children singing as they walk · 50
Riding a water buffalo cart for the first time · 54 I will protect you, little brother · 56
A refugee camp school where friendship grows · 58
With ardent eyes · 62 With dreams carried on a boat · 64
Cave houses in the submerged ancient city of Hasankeyf · 66
On a wrecked Israeli tank · 70 Flowers instead of bombs · 74 A warrior's daughter · 76
A shoemaker at Peshawar Market · 78 Children making bricks · 80
In the desert at sunset · 82 Waiting for spring · 86 Holding a lamb · 88
Forever, Che Guevara · 90 Pashtun girls · 92 Pashtun boys · 94
Run, children · 96 Carrying date palms · 100 Good friends, even just looking · 102
The Untouchable boy's prayer · 104 Once round the neighborhood · 106
Children are amazing · 108

Biography · 113
Books · 116

서문 · 9

작품

길 떠나는 소년 · 18 감자를 굽는 아이들 · 22 멋쟁이 어린 농부 · 24

벼 타작하는 날 · 26 저 산 너머엔 · 28 헤브론 광야의 소년들 · 32

동생을 등에 업고 · 34 씨앗을 지키는 아이 · 36 브란따 항구의 어부 가족 · 38

목욕하는 형제 · 40 양동이 지게를 지고 · 44 로띠를 굽는 시간 · 46

탐빈나무 숲에서 · 48 노래하며 가는 아이들 · 50 물소 수레를 처음 탄 날 · 54

누나가 지켜줄게 · 56 우정이 자라는 난민촌 학교 · 58 간절한 눈빛으로 · 62

조각배에 꿈을 싣고 · 64 수몰된 고대 도시 하산케이프의 동굴집 · 66

파괴된 이스라엘 탱크 위에서 · 70 폭탄 대신 꽃을 · 74

전사의 딸 · 76 페샤와르 시장의 신발 수선공 · 78 흙벽돌 찍는 아이들 · 80

노을 지는 사막에서 · 82 봄을 기다리며 · 86 어린 양을 안고 · 88

영원하라, 체 게바라 · 90 파슈툰 소녀들 · 92 파슈툰 소년들 · 94

달려라 아이들아 · 96 대추야자를 운반하며 · 100 바라만 봐도 좋은 친구 · 102

불가촉천민 소년의 기도 · 104 둥글게 동네 한 바퀴 · 106

아이들은 놀라워라 · 108

약력 · 113
저서 · 116

지구에서 좋은 게 뭐죠?
아이, 아이, 아이들요.
하늘같이 맑은 눈의 아이들요.

아이들 앞에 서면, 나는 두 가지 감정에 사로잡힌다. 그것은 '놀라움'과 '두려움'이다. "가난하여도 지혜로운 아이는 앞날을 내다볼 줄 모르는 나이 들고 어리석은 왕보다 훌륭하다."(전도서 4:13) 아이들이 나를 바라보고 있다. 하늘같이 맑은 눈의 아이들이. 그 천진한 눈망울이 내게는 가장 떨리고 엄중한 시선이다. 행여 아이들에게 나쁜 영향을 미치지 않을까, 나쁜 길을 선보이지 않을까, 나는 내 삶의 태도와 말과 행동과 걸음을 가다듬는다.
　인간 세상에 가슴 두근거리는 기적이 있다면, 그것은 아이, 아이들의 탄생이 아닌가. 우리에게 남은 희망이 있다면, '나 여기 왔어요' 세상에 고하는 아이의 첫 울음이 아닌가. 지구 위에 아이 한 명이 탄생하는 순간, 또 하나의 목소리가, 또 하나의 세계가, 새로운 희망과 사랑이 시작된다. 그것은 결코 반복의 역사가 아니다. 아이들은 미래에서 온 빛이고 미래로 난 길이다. 낡아진 관습의 굴레에 필사적으로 반항하고 저항하며 오늘의 진보한 세계를 진부하게 만들고, 확고하던 질서에 균열을 내며 그냥 앞으로, 낯설고 새로운 길로 내딛어 나아가버린다. 아이들은 가장 위대한 '창조적 배반자'이고 그로부터 인류의 희망과 세상의 혁명은 대를 이어 계속되어 왔으니.

이 지상에서 아이에게 첫 만남의 존재이자 삶에 결정적인 영향을 주는 최초의 세계는 부모이다. 하여 '엄마, 아빠'라는 부름은 '인생의 축복'이자 '고통의 성직聖職'이다. 아이들의 먹을 것을 구하고자 끝없는 노동과 남모를 수모를 감내하며, 그래도 너는 나를 딛고 나아가라고 헌신하는 그 애타는 마음을 안다. 그러나 이 사진 속 세계의 절반이 넘는 아이들에 비추어볼 때, 슬프게도, 지금 우리 아이들의 심신은 갈수록 허약해지고 있다. 지금 우리 아이들은 너무나 과잉 개발되고 있다. 모든 게 짜여지고 계획되고 들어차고 여백과 여지가 남아있지 않아 아이들의 영혼은 숨이 죽어간다.

역사에서 처음으로 맞이하는 이 과잉의 시대에, 우리가 해야 할 단 하나가 있다면 아이들에게 '존재의 광활함'을 허용하는 일이다. 결여 속에 살아나는 간절함과 강인함, 자연 속에 깨어나는 전인적 감각, 순수한 우정의 친구, 모험과 분투, 침잠과 고독, 시련과 상처까지, 그러니까 자유, 자유의 공기 말이다. 아이는 부모라는 지구 인간의 몸을 타고 여기 왔으나 온 우주를 한껏 머금은 장엄한 존재이다. 아무도 모른다. 이 아이가 누구이고, 왜 이곳에 왔고, 그 무엇이 되어 어디로 나아갈지. 지금 작고 갓난해도 영원으로부터 온 아이는 이미 다 가지고 여기 왔으니.

우리 모두는 아이였다. 나이가 들고 어른이 되어도 죽는 날까지 우리 안에는 소년 소녀가 살아있다. 너무 짧고 괴로운 이 한 생에서, 우리 모두는 상처 난 아이다. 저 우주의 별빛과 하늘의 눈빛 앞에서, 우리 모두는 언제까지나 아이다. 늘 모자라고 서투르고 실수하고 그럼에도 거듭 배우고 성찰하며 다시 깨달아가야 하는 우리 모두는 '영원의 아이'다.

여기 병들어가는 지구 위에서, 그래도 아이들이 태어나고 아이들이 자라나고 있다. 이 지구별 위를 잠시 동행하는 아이들에게 나는 한 사람의 좋은 벗이 되어주고, '뜨거운 믿음의 침묵'으로 눈물의 기도를 바칠 뿐이니.

아이야, 착하고 강하여라.
사랑이 많고 지혜로워라.
아름답고 생생하여라.
맘껏 뛰놀고 기뻐하고 감사하며
네 삶을 망치는 것들과 싸워가라.
언제까지나 네 마음 깊은 곳에
하늘 빛과 힘이 끊이지 않기를.
네가 여기 와주어 감사하다. 사랑한다.

2022년 9월
박노해

What's good on Earth?

Children, children, children.

Children with eyes clear as the sky.

When I stand before children, I am caught up in two emotions, 'surprise' and 'fear.' "It is better to be a poor but wise youth than an old and foolish king who refuses to look ahead."(Ecclesiastes 4:13) Children look at me. Children with eyes clear as the sky. Those innocent eyes are the most sensitive and strictest gaze to me. Wondering if I have had a bad influence on children or shown them a bad way, I adjust my attitude, words, actions, and steps in my life.

If there is any miracle in the human world that makes our hearts flutter, isn't it a child, the birth of children? If there is any hope left for us, isn't it the first cry of a child saying 'I'm here' to the world? The moment a child is born on the earth, another voice, another world, new hope and love begin. It is by no means a history of repetitions. Children are light from the future and the path to the future. Desperately rebelling against and resisting the yoke of outdated customs, making today's advanced world banal, making the established order crack, they simply advance along unfamiliar, new paths. Children are the greatest 'creative traitors,' and thanks to them human hopes and the world's revolutions have continued from generation to generation.

Parents are the first beings that children meet on this earth and the first world that has a decisive influence on their lives. Therefore, being called 'Mom, Dad' is a 'blessing of life' and a 'vocation to pain.' You endure endless labors and humiliations that no one knows in order to obtain food for your children, but you have anxious hearts that urge you to advance, sacrificing yourselves. But thinking of more than half the world's children seen in these pictures, sadly, nowadays our children's minds and bodies are getting weaker and weaker. Our children are now too overdeveloped. Everything is crafted, organized, planned, filled, so that there is no space or room left, the children's souls are suffocating.

In this age of excess, for the first time in history, if there is only one thing we have to do, it is to allow children 'a vastness of being.' Ardor and strength surviving in lack, a holistic sense awaking in nature, friends in pure affection, adventure and struggle, deep thought and solitude, trials and wounds, that is, freedom, the air of freedom. The child came here to the Earth by a human body called the parent, but it is a majestic being that embraces the whole universe to its fullest. Nobody knows who this child is, why he is here, what he will be and where he will go. Even if small and newborn now, the child arriving from eternity came bringing everything.

We were all children. Even when we grow up and become adults, the little boy or girl lives in us until the day we die. In this very short and painful life, we are all wounded children. Before the starlight of the universe and the eyes of the sky, we are all children, forever. We are all 'eternal children,' who are always deficient, clumsy, make mistakes, and have to learn, reflect, and realize over and over again.

Here on this ailing planet, children are still being born and children are growing up. I am a good friend to the children who accompany me on this planet for a while, and I simply pray with tears in the 'hot silence of faith.'

Child, be good and strong.
Be loving and wise.
Be beautiful and lively.
Run freely, rejoice and be grateful.
Fight the things that ruin your life.
May the light and strength of heaven
never leave the depths of your heart.
Thank you for coming here. I love you.

September, 2022
Park Nohae

길 떠나는 소년

안데스 산맥의 높고 외딴 집에 사는 모자가
이른 아침부터 감자를 싣고 먼 길을 떠난다.
일찍이 아빠를 잃은 열한 살 로니 일레메는
물려받은 낡은 손목시계에서 아빠를 느낀다.
"제가 아홉 살이 됐을 때 엄마가 채워주셨어요.
'이 시계를 찰 때가 되면 네가 집안의 가장이다.
아빠는 하늘에서도 너와 엄마를 지켜줄 것이고
파차마마와 모든 신들이 널 보살펴줄 것이다.
아들아, 미안하다. 착하고 강하게 살아가라.'
아빠가 제게 남기신 마지막 말씀이래요."
어린 가장은 말에 맨 밧줄을 팽팽히 당기며
흐르는 시간 속을 힘차게 걸어간다.

A BOY SETTING OFF ON A JOURNEY

A mother and her son, who live in a high-up, isolated house in the Andes,
set off on a long journey in the early morning with a load of potatoes.
Eleven-year-old Ronnie Ileme, who lost his father at an early age,
feels his father in the worn-out wristwatch that he has inherited.
"Mom gave it to me when I turned nine. 'It's time for you to wear this watch,
that means you are the head of this household. From Heaven, Dad will protect
you and your Mom, Pachamama and all the gods will take care of you.
Son, I'm sorry. Live a good and strong life.' She said those were the last words
my father left me." The young family head walks vigorously through
passing time, pulling firmly on the rope tied to the horse.

On the way to Ancasi, Cusco, Peru, 2010.

감 자 를 굽 는 아 이 들

오늘은 감자를 수확하는 두레 노동의 날.
일하는 어른들 곁에서 아이들도 바쁜 하루다.
야생화 언덕 사이로 신나게 뛰어놀다가,
말에게 풀도 뜯기고 어린 동생들을 돌보다가,
날이 저물 녘이면 마른 풀을 모아 불을 피우고
저녁 식탁에 오를 갓 캐낸 감자를 굽는다.
고생 끝에 맛있게 구워낸 감자를 나눠먹으며
'장하다, 애썼다, 고맙다'는 어른들의 칭찬과 격려는
아이들의 작은 가슴을 자긍심으로 부풀게 한다.

CHILDREN BAKING POTATOES

Today is the day for the cooperative to harvest potatoes. The children are
busy alongside the working adults. They run about happily among hills
full of wild flowers, give the horses grass and take care of their younger siblings,
then at sunset, they gather dry grass, light a fire and bake freshly dug potatoes
for the dinner table. Sharing delicious baked potatoes after hard work,
the compliments and encouragement of the adults, saying, 'You've worked hard,
great, thank you,' make the children's little breasts swell with pride.

Patacancha, Cusco, Peru, 2010.

멋쟁이 어린 농부

내리쬐는 햇볕과 만년설산 찬바람 속에
머리를 보호하는 모자는 안데스의 필수품이다.
할아버지가 아빠에게 물려준 모자는 이제
일을 거들기 시작한 아들의 것이 되었다.
나도 안데스의 농부라는 듯 멋지게 모자를 갖춰 쓰고
제 몸만 한 괭이를 든 아이의 품새가 제법 단단하다.
이 땅을 지켜갈 아이들과 그 아이들의 아이들이
대를 이어 자라나고 이어지고 있다는 것,
그것이 우리 희망의 근거가 아닌가.

A HANDSOME YOUNG FARMER

A hat that protects the head from the scorching sun and the cold wind of
the snowy mountains is a must in the Andes. The hat his grandfather passed
down to his father now belongs to the son, who is just beginning to help.
As if to show that he too is a farmer in the Andes, a child smartly wearing
a hat and holding a hoe as tall as himself stands firmly. That the children who
will protect this land and the children of those children are growing and
handing it down from generation to generation, is surely the basis of our hope.

Patacancha, Cusco, Peru, 2010.

벼 타 작 하 는 날

마을 사람들이 모여 벼 타작을 하는 날에는
아이들도 학교 대신 논에 나와 일을 거든다.
소년은 볏단을 옮기며 한 사람 몫을 든든히 해낸다.
"저, 비밀인데요. 처음엔 힘들어서 눈물 날 뻔했어요.
그래도 어깨너머로 따라 배우고 요령도 생기면서
내가 이만큼 해냈구나, 신도 나고 힘이 나요."
노동과 놀이와 공부가 하나 된 삶의 현장에서
온몸으로 살아 움직이며 자라나는 아이들.
어렸을 때부터 대지와 이웃 속에서 자연스레
전승되고 익혀가는 현장 지성과 전인적 감각은
생애 내내 부닥치는 삶의 문제와 자기 결정에
무능하지 않은 고귀한 밑거름이 되어주리니.

RICE THRESHING DAY

On days when villagers gather to thresh rice, the children also come to
the rice fields to help instead of going to school. One boy moves the rice
sheaves and does his job well. "Well, it's a secret. At first, it was so difficult
that I almost cried. Still, I learned by watching others and gained skills,
so now I've accomplished this much, I'm thrilled and grow stronger."
These children live and grow utterly immersed in the field of life where work,
play and study are united. The practical intelligence and holistic sense that
are naturally handed down and learned from childhood on the land and
in the neighborhood will serve as a noble foundation throughout their life so
as not to be incompetent faced with life's problems and for self-determination.

Sargodha, Punjab, Pakistan, 2011.

BEYOND THAT MOUNTAIN

The path along which dogs and donkeys with bells ringing go out
together to highlands green with the fresh springing grass that
the flocks of sheep love. The older sister puts a blanket in case
rain filled wind blows, boiled potatoes, cheese, and coca leaves in
a cloth and ties it tightly on her back. The younger brother, going out
for the first time, follows her, growing familiar with the path.
"What is beyond that mountain, that hill? Someday I want to travel
far away into a wider world." As if the rhythm of the Andes was
already borne in the melody of her body, the girl gently climbs the slope.

Palccayme, Cusco, Peru, 2010.

저 산 너 머 엔

양떼가 좋아하는 새 풀이 돋아난 푸른 고원으로
강아지도 당나귀도 방울소리 울리며 함께 나서는 길.
누나는 비바람이 불면 둘러쓸 담요, 삶은 감자와 치즈
그리고 코카잎까지 보자기에 싸 야무지게 등에 메고,
처음 나선 동생은 길을 익히며 뒤따라간다.
"저 산 저 언덕 저 너머엔 무엇이 있을까요.
언젠간 더 큰 세상으로 멀리멀리 가보고 싶어요."
안데스의 리듬이 이미 몸의 선율로 실려있는 듯
소녀는 사뿐사뿐 비탈길을 오른다.

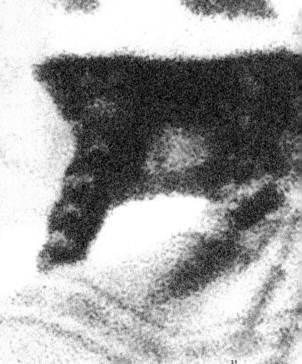

헤브론 광야의 소년들

광야에 첫 비가 내리고 풀빛이 싱그러울 때
아이들은 양떼를 몰며 '걷는 독서'를 한다.
성서에도 기록된 고원지대 헤브론은 물이 넉넉하고
포도와 올리브, 벌꿀과 무화과가 풍성한 땅이지만
지금은 점령당한 분쟁의 땅이 되고 말았다.
그래도 양떼는 풀을 뜯고 아이들은 책을 읽는다.
비록 내일이면 여린 손에 작은 돌멩이를 쥐고
침략자의 탱크를 향해 달려갈지라도.

BOYS IN THE HEBRON WILDERNESS

When the first rain falls in the wilderness and the grass is fresh,
the children herd sheep and practice "reading while walking along."
The Hebron highlands, mentioned in the Bible, are a land of abundant
waters, rich in grapes, olives, honey, and figs. It has now become an
occupied land of strife. Still, the sheep graze and the children read books.
Even if tomorrow they will run towards the invader's tanks
holding small stones in their tender hands.

Hebron, Palestine, 2008.

동생을 등에 업고

고산 마을에서 한 뼘의 밭이라도 넓히기 위해
마을 어른들은 멀리 산 위로 길을 떠나고,
소녀가 울며 보채는 동생을 등에 업고 달랜다.
막대사탕을 건네자 동생 입에만 물려준다.
"저는 괜찮아요. 동생을 내려 놓으면 울거든요.
갓난아기 때부터 제 등에 업고 잠을 재웠어요.
이제는 등에 업힌 동생이 배고픈지, 졸린지,
아니면 어디가 아픈지 전 다 알 수 있어요."
아, 우리들은 다 이렇게 부모님과 언니 누나의
등에 업혀 자라나 지금 이 지상을 걷고 있으니.

CARRYING HER LITTLE BROTHER
ON HER BACK

High in the hills, in order to expand a field even by just a span, the village
elders set off up a distant mountain, and a girl carries her crying little brother
on her back to comfort him. I gave her a lollipop, she puts it in her brother's
mouth. "I'm OK. If I put my brother down he cries. I've been putting him to
sleep on my back since he was a baby. Now I can tell if my brother on my back
is hungry, sleepy, or sick." Ah, we all grew up on the backs of our parents
and older sisters, and now we are walking on this earth.

Phunoi village, Boun Neua, Phongsali, Laos, 2011.

씨 앗 을 지 키 는 아 이

마을 어디서나 보이는 중심 자리에
한 생을 마친 수백 년 된 고목 위로
다음 생을 이어갈 종자 싹이 트고 있다.
결실은 아래로 고르게 나눠져야 하지만
고귀한 종자는 높은 곳에 두어야 한다.
높은 곳은 더 춥고 척박하고 고독할지라도
태양과 별들이 그를 품고 단련해주는 곳.
그리하여 마침내 새날의 희망이 되는 것.
아이가 정성스런 손길로 종자 싹을 가꾼다.

A CHILD TENDING SEEDS

In the center of the village, visible from anywhere in the village, seeds that
will continue a new life are sprouting on top of a tree that is hundreds of
years old and at the end of its life. The fruit should be taken down and
evenly divided, but the noblest seeds should be placed high up. Even though
the high places are colder, barren, and lonely, that's a place where the sun and
stars embrace and train them. So, finally they become the hope of a new day.
A child tends the seed buds with careful hands.

Akha Phixor village, Ban Phapoun Mai, Phongsali, Laos, 2011.

브란따 항구의 어부 가족

거센 파도를 헤치고 고깃배가 돌아오면
아이들은 벌써 항구로 달려나간다.
아빠가 잡은 신선한 생선을 배에서 건네주면
종류별로 바구니에 담는 것은 아이의 일이다.
가정이란 부모든 아이든 누구 한 사람을
중심으로 돌아가는 곳이 아니다.
성장단계에 따라 저마다 기여할 몫이 있고,
서로 헌신하는 만큼 함께 향유하며
하나의 믿음 속에 각자의 꿈을 꾸는 곳.
스스로 자기 앞가림을 해나가는 습관과
함께 살아가는 인간의 도리를 배우는 곳.
가정은 아이에게 있어 최초의 공동체이고
좋은 세상을 향한 첫 번째 출발지이다.

FISHERMEN'S FAMILY AT BRANTA HARBOR

When the fishing boat returns after breaking through the strong waves,
the children are already running to the port. It is the children's job to take the fresh
fish caught by their father from the boat and put them in baskets according to type.
A home is not a place that revolves around just one person, parent or child.
It's a place where each person has a share to contribute according to their age,
a place where they enjoy being together, dedicated to each other and each dream
their own dreams united in trust. A place where they learn the habit of taking care
of themselves and the ways of the human beings living together. The family is
the child's first community, the first point of departure towards a better world.

Pamekasan, Madura Island, East Java, Indonesia, 2013.

BROTHERS TAKING A BATH

A village along the River Irrawaddy where daily workers live in huts.
The riverside here is a communal launderette and open-air bathroom.
It is a news source for adults and a playground for children.
While mother, returning from her work, washes off the sweat and
does the laundry, the older brother rubs his younger brother's back
with the precious piece of soap he's been using. "I had an argument
with my brother today, but we reconciled by rubbing each other's back.
When mother only takes care of my little brother, I feel a bit upset.
When that happens, I secretly go off to the market with my friends.
Ha ha. If I had been an only child without a younger brother,
I would have felt lonely and cramped." Disappointments, lacks,
and sorrows all flow away in the river. The brothers will fall asleep
to the sound of the water and have dreams like starlight.

River Irrawaddy, Mandalay, Burma, 2011.

목욕하는 형제

일용직 노동자들이 움막을 치고 사는 이라와디 마을.
이곳 강변은 공동 빨래방이자 노천 목욕탕이고
어른들의 소식터이자 아이들의 놀이터이다.
일을 마치고 돌아온 엄마가 땀을 씻고 빨래를 하는 동안
형은 아껴 쓰던 귀한 비누조각으로 동생의 등을 밀어준다.
"오늘 동생이랑 다퉜는데 서로 등 밀어주면서 화해했어요.
엄마가 동생만 챙겨줄 때는 좀 속상하기도 한데요,
그럴 땐 몰래 친구들이랑 장에도 쏘다니고 그래요. 하하.
동생 없이 저 혼자였으면 외롭고 갑갑했을 것 같아요."
아쉬움도 모자람도 서운함도 강물에 흘려 보내고
형제는 물소리에 잠이 들어 별빛같은 꿈을 꾸겠다.

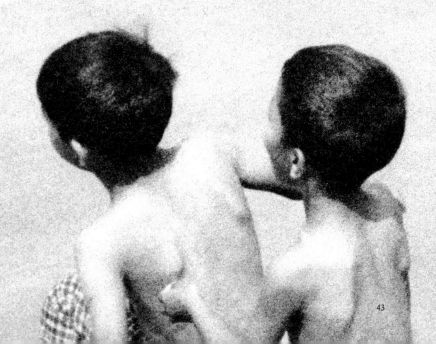

양동이 지게를 지고

온 가족이 벼를 수확하고 정미하는 날,
소년은 양동이 지게에 쌀겨를 지고 나른다.
인도에서 볏짚과 쌀겨는 가축의 먹이로도 쓰고,
소똥에 섞어 말려 연료로 쓰고, 흙집 보수에도 쓴다.
이 작은 아이는 벌써 할 줄 아는 게 참 많다.
밥을 차려 먹고 청소하고 이불 개고 심부름하고
손님이 오면 차를 내고 곁에 앉아 귀 기울이고.
아이들은 이렇게 삶 속에서 저절로 배워간다.
교육은 삶에 대한 태도에서 시작되는 것.
아니, 삶 그 자체에서 교육은 완성되는 것.
볏짚을 먹은 소가 우유를 주고
쌀겨를 먹은 닭이 달걀을 주면
새 신발을 살 생각에 땀 젖은 얼굴엔 웃음이 돌고
발걸음은 힘차고 경쾌하기만 하다.

CARRYING BUCKETS

On the day the whole family harvests and polishes the rice, the boy carries
the rice bran in buckets. In India, rice straw and rice bran are used as feed
for livestock, mixed with cow dung and dried to be used as fuel, and used to
repair mud houses. This little kid already knows how to do a lot of things.
He cooks and eats rice, cleans, folds blankets, runs errands, and when guests
arrive, he makes tea, then sits down and listens carefully. In this way children
learn naturally in life. Education begins with an attitude towards life.
Indeed, education is completed in life itself. When a cow that eats rice straw
gives milk or a chicken that eats rice bran gives eggs, a sweaty face smiles at
the thought of buying new shoes, his steps are strong and cheerful.

Auli village, Orissa, India, 2013.

로띠를 굽는 시간

집집마다 화덕에 하얀 연기가 피어오르고
갓 구운 고소한 빵 냄새가 퍼져나가는 저녁.
직접 씨 뿌려 거둔 햇밀로 만든 반죽을
무쇠판에 올려 로띠를 굽는 엄마 곁에서
아이는 불을 때고 조절하는 일을 돕는다.
"하루 중에 제일 행복한 시간이에요.
아이와 오늘 있었던 일을 나누며 말해주죠.
누구든 만나면 먼저 웃으며 인사하렴.
친구와 우애 깊은 사람이 진짜 부자란다.
거짓말하면 네 마음이 불편하니 정직하렴.
그리고 늘 감사한 마음으로 살아가렴."

TIME TO BAKE ROTI

In the evening, white smoke rises from the fire in every house and the
delicious smell of freshly baked bread spreads. A child helps to light and
control the fire next to its mother who bakes the roti by putting dough
made from fresh wheat she sowed and harvested herself on a cast iron plate.
"It is the happiest time of the day. I talk to our child about what happened
today. I tell him, when you meet someone, greet them with a smile first.
People with deep affection for friends are truly rich. If you tell lies,
you feel bad, so be honest. And always live with a grateful heart."

Bahawalpur, Punjab, Pakistan, 2011.

탐 빈 나 무 숲 에 서

7년 동안 뿌리와 밑둥만 키우다 약 3미터가 되면
30미터 높이까지 자라나는 버마의 탐빈나무.
꼭대기에 달린 열매 줄기에서 채취한 수액 탕예는
달고 시원한 음료이자 술과 원당의 원재료다.
수액 통을 가지러 맨발로 나무에 오른 아빠를
조마조마하며 어깨 걸고 지켜보고 있는 남매.
이 마을 아이들에게 진정한 어른이 된다는 것은
탐빈나무에 오를 힘과 용기를 갖게 되는 것이다.
"아빠가 멋있어요. 저도 어서 커서 나무에 올라
높은 곳에서 세상을 보고 탕예를 가져올 거예요."
아이들의 존경과 응원에 아빠는 더욱 힘을 내는
키 큰 탐빈나무 숲은 외롭지 않은 일터다.

IN A TODDY PALM GROVE

The toddy palm trees in Myanmar grow to a height of up to 30 meters
after first growing roots and base to about 3 meters high for 7 years.
The sap collected from the stems of the fruit hanging at the top is a sweet,
refreshing drink, and is a raw material for producing liquor and raw sugar.
A brother and sister anxiously watch their dad, who is climbing a tree
barefoot to collect the sap bottles. For the children of this village,
becoming a real adult means having the strength and courage to climb
the toddy palm trees. "Dad is great. I want to grow up quickly, and climb
trees to see the world from a high place and bring down the sap."
The grove of tall trees, where the father receives extra strength from
the children's respect and support, is a workplace where he is not lonely.

Nyaung-U, Bagan, Burma, 2011.

CHILDREN SINGING
AS THEY WALK

4,000 meters above sea level in the breathtaking
Simien Mountains children carry on their heads branches
that are heavier than themselves. They walk a long way,
heading for a marketplace on the plateau. After selling
a piece of wood they hold only 30 cents in their hand.
But the children sing in clear, high-pitched voices.
Hope, as much as the weight that burdens them,
makes them sing an octave higher and think one octave up.
Right, children, you're small now, but you're already big.
You are burdened now, but light is coming ahead of you.
You do not know it now, but your time is coming.

Simien Mountains, Ethiopia, 2008.

노래하며 가는 아이들

숨이 가쁜 해발 4천미터 시미엔 산맥 길에서
아이들이 제 몸무게보다 무거운 나뭇짐을 이고
먼 길을 걸어 고원의 장터로 향한다.
나뭇짐을 팔아 손에 쥐는 건 단돈 300원인데,
아이들은 맑고 높은 목소리로 노래를 부른다.
희망은, 자신을 짓누르는 무게만큼
한 옥타브 높은 목소리로 노래하고
한 옥타브 위의 사고를 해야 한다는 듯이.
그래 아이야, 너는 지금 작지만 너는 이미 크다.
너는 지금 무겁지만 네 앞에는 빛이 온다.
너는 지금 모르지만 너의 때가 오고 있다.

물 소 수 레 를 처 음 탄 날

농사를 도와주고 짐수레를 끌어주는 물소는
버마인들에게 고마운 식구이고 친구이다.
여섯 살 소년 텟은 오늘 처음 물소 고삐를 쥐었다.
소달구지의 조정법을 알려주는 아빠의 말을 따라
아이는 바닥에 깔아놓은 콩 위를 둥그레 돌며
작은 사령관이 된 듯 물소를 이끌어간다.
노동을 하는 가축도 나눠먹을 권리가 있다며
입망을 씌우지 않고 콩을 먹게 하는 그 마음까지,
아이는 더불어 살아가는 법을 배워간다.

RIDING A WATER BUFFALO CART
FOR THE FIRST TIME

The buffalo, who helps with farming and pulls carts, is a much-appreciated family member and friend to the Burmese. Today, six-year-old Tet is holding the bridle of a water buffalo for the first time. Following his father's instructions on how to drive the oxcart, the child directs the buffalo as if he were a small commander, turning in circles on the beans spread on the ground. The child learns how to live together, even allowing it to eat some of the beans without restraining it, sensing that working livestock have the right to eat their share.

Innwa, Mandalay, Burma, 2011.

누나가 지켜 줄 게

막막한 사막 지평과 불타는 태양 볕에
누비아 사막엔 태초의 정적만이 흐른다.
아빠는 낙타에 대추야자를 싣고 떠났다.
며칠째 아빠가 무사히 돌아오기를 기다리는 남매는
시원한 흙집을 두고 불볕의 사막을 서성인다.
"내 손 놓으면 안 돼, 누나가 지켜줄게."
이글거리는 사막의 맹수가 걱정되는 누나는
다섯 살 남동생의 손을 꼬옥 잡는다.
사랑은 한 인간으로서 약함과 결여로부터 나온다.
'나는 네가 필요하다. 네가 함께 있어주면 좋겠다.
그런 너를 위해 나 또한 너에게 나를 내어주겠다'는
그 사랑의 힘으로 우리는 나아가는 것이니.

I WILL PROTECT YOU, LITTLE BROTHER

With the barren desert horizon and the burning sun, in the Nubian desert nothing but a primeval silence reigns. Dad has gone off with a date palm loaded on a camel. Sister and brother, after waiting for their father to return safely for the past several days, leave the cool earthen house and go wandering across the scorching desert. "You mustn't let go of my hand, I will protect you." Worried about the glaring desert beasts, the older sister holds her five-year-old brother's hand tightly. Love comes from a human being's weakness and lack. "I need you. I am glad you are with me. For your sake, I will also give myself to you," with the power of that love we are moving forward.

Old Dongola, Nubian, Sudan, 2008.

A REFUGEE CAMP SCHOOL
WHERE FRIENDSHIP GROWS

An old blackboard in front of a dented mud wall. There are no classrooms
or desks sheltered from the scorching sunlight, but the children in Afghan
refugee camps, even the younger siblings, walk a long way to school.
Children come to school with so much enthusiasm, not just to learn
arithmetic or letters. It's because the day is busy, collecting some of
the bread bought for lunch, then going to the house of a friend who stepped
on a landmine a while ago, bringing together children who quarreled helping
them shake hands in reconciliation, and let's fly a kite, let's play hoop,
let's play soccer, let's go pick some grapes to eat. Children simply grow up
on their own when they are with nature and their friends, playing, fighting,
reconciling, helping, competing, collaborating, learning from each other
and leaning on each other. The greatest virtue that school can give is
an opportunity to meet and build such friendships.

Mardan, Khyber Pakhtunkhwa, Pakistan, 2011.

우정이 자라는 난민촌 학교

패인 흙담 앞에 다 낡은 칠판 하나,
따가운 햇빛을 피할 교실도 책상도 없지만
아프간 난민촌 아이들은 어린 동생들까지
데리고 먼 길을 걸어 학교에 나온다.
아이들이 이렇게나 열성으로 학교에 오는 건
산술이나 글자를 배우기 위해서만이 아니다.
점심으로 싸온 빵을 조금씩 떼어 모아서
얼마 전 지뢰를 밟은 친구네 집을 찾아가고,
싸운 애들을 모아 화해의 악수를 시키고,
'연 날리러 가자, 굴렁쇠 하자, 축구 하자,
포도 따 먹으러 가자' 하루가 바쁘기 때문이다.
아이들은 그저 자연과 친구들과 있으면
놀고 싸우고 화해하고 돕고 경쟁하고 협력하고
그렇게 서로 배우고 기대며 스스로 자란다.
학교가 줄 수 있는 최고의 미덕은
그런 우정을 쌓아갈 만남의 기회인 것을.

간절한 눈빛으로

지도에도 없는 높고 깊은 산속의 아카족 마을.
보아주는 이 없어도 정성껏 전통 의상을 차려 입고
판자로 지은 한 칸짜리 학교에 모여든 아이들이
아빠들이 짜준 나무 책상에 앉자마자
간절한 눈동자로 공부 삼매경에 빠져든다.
배움은 간절함이다.
결핍과 결여만이 줄 수 있는 간절함이다.
그 간절함이 궁리와 창의, 도전과 분투,
견디는 힘과 강인한 삶의 의지를 불어넣는다.
우리가 아이들에게서 빼앗아버린 것은
그 소중한 '결여'와 '여백'이 아닌가.
간절한 마음에 빛과 힘이 온다.

WITH ARDENT EYES

An Akha village that is high up, deep in the hills, not on any map. Even if there is no one to look after them, the children in traditional costumes with ardent eyes who gather in the one-room school made of boards are absorbed in study as soon as they sit down at the wooden desks their fathers made. Learning is ardor. It is the ardor that only want and lack can give. Such ardor inspires ingenuity and creativity, challenges and struggles, endurance and a strong will to live. Isn't it the precious 'lack' and 'blank space' that we have taken away from our children? Light and strength come to ardent hearts.

Akha Phixor village, Ban Phapoun Mai, Phongsali, Laos, 2011.

조각배에 꿈을 싣고

고원에 자리한 '산 위의 바다' 인레 호수는
아름다운 자연과 여러 민족의 전통문화가
생생하게 살아있어 '버마의 심장'이라 불린다.
그러나 군부 쿠데타로 지금은 갈 수 없는 땅.
물결만이 자유로이 흘러가는 인레에서
아홉 살 소년이 동생을 학교에 데려다주러
조각배에 태우고 능숙하게 발로 노를 젓는다.
인생은 고통의 바다라지만
그래도 우리는 나아가리라.
바람과 파도가 단련시킨 그 힘으로.
한 배를 타고 동행하는 믿음과 희망으로.

WITH DREAMS CARRIED ON A BOAT

Lake Inle, the 'sea above the mountain,' located on a plateau, is called
'the heart of Burma' because of its beautiful nature and the traditional
culture of various ethnic groups. However, due to the military coup d'état,
it cannot be visited now. In Inle, where only the waves flow freely,
a nine-year-old boy takes his younger brother to school in a boat, skillfully
paddling with his feet. Life is a sea of suffering, but we will move ahead.
With the strength that the wind and waves have forged.
With faith and hope traveling together in one boat.

Lake Inle, Nyaung Shwe, Burma, 2011.

CAVE HOUSES IN THE SUBMERGED
ANCIENT CITY OF HASANKEYF

Hasankeyf, an ancient city with a history of 8,000 years belonging
to the Kurds, the world's largest ethnic minority who have lost their country.
It is full of ruins from Sumer, Rome, and the Ottoman Empire, and it is also
the home of the Kurdish people's shining life. However, the Turkish government
built a dam upstream on the Tigris River to drown Hasankeyf in 2020.
The cave houses containing thousands of years of Kurdish wisdom
and the laughter of children playing hide-and-seek have disappeared.
However, the noble things engraved on the hearts of the children
will not disappear, but will be remembered and passed on to the future.

Hasankeyf, Kurdistan, Turkiye, 2006.

수몰된 고대 도시 하산케이프의 동굴집

나라 잃은 세계 최대 소수민족 쿠르드인들의
8천년 역사가 어린 고대 도시 하산케이프.
수메르, 로마, 오스만 제국 등의 유적이 가득하고
쿠르드인들의 빛나는 삶의 터전이기도 하다.
그러나 터키 정부는 티그리스 강 상류에 댐을 지어
2020년에 이곳 하산케이프를 수장하고 말았다.
쿠르드인들의 수천 년 지혜가 담긴 동굴집들도
숨바꼭질하던 아이들의 웃음소리도 사라져버렸다.
그러나 아이들의 가슴에 새겨진 고귀한 것들은
사라지지 않고 미래로 기억되고 이어져갈 테니.

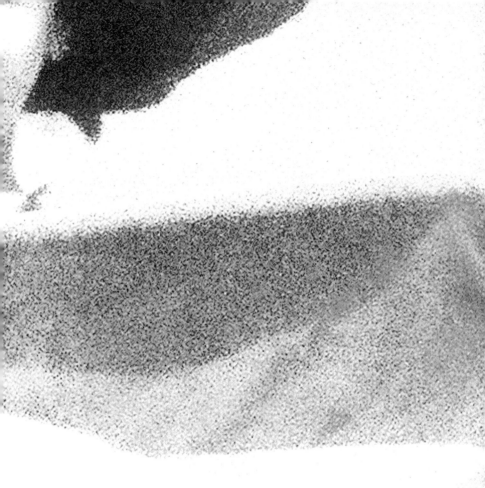

ON A WRECKED ISRAELI TANK

In 2006, Israel invaded Lebanon. The border town of Bint Jubail
was a tomb of ruins. On top of an Israeli tank that was stopped in
a life-and-death battle, waving a Lebanese flag and a Hezbollah flag,
tearful ten-year-old Ali and seven-year-old Gadir. When they returned
from evacuation, their house, school, and friends were gone.
"What are you doing up there on that tank?" "Letting our dead friends
in heaven see us. Sarah, Hussein, Hassan··· sleep peacefully.
Don't wake up to the sound of bombs, don't cry because you're scared···
we'll not forget, we will remember you, let's meet again."
There are children whose dream is life, to live and not die.

Bint Jubail, Lebanon, 2006.

파괴된 이스라엘 탱크 위에서

이스라엘이 레바논을 침공한 2006년,
국경 마을 빈트 주베일은 폐허의 무덤이었다.
목숨 건 항전으로 멈춰 세운 이스라엘 탱크 위에서
레바논 국기와 헤즈볼라 깃발을 흔들며
울먹이는 열 살 알리와 일곱 살 가디르 남매.
피난 갔다 돌아오니 집도 학교도 친구들도 사라져버렸다.
"왜 탱크 위에서 그러고 있니?"
"죽은 친구들이 하늘나라에서 보라구요.
사라, 후세인, 하산… 편히 잠들어.
폭탄소리에도 깨어나지 말고, 무섭다고 울지 말고….
잊지 않고 기억할게. 우리 다시 만나자."
죽지 않고 사는 게, 살아있는 게 꿈인 아이들이 있다.

폭탄 대신 꽃을

이스라엘 전폭기의 집중 폭격으로
황무지처럼 무너져버린 스리파 마을.
마을 축제를 앞두고 연극 연습을 하던
많은 아이들이 한 자리에서 숨졌다.
살아남은 소녀들이 버려진 조화를 들고 와
내 손을 이끌더니 사진을 찍어 달란다.
친구들이 죽은 자리에 꽃을 들고 서서
참아온 슬픔을 터뜨리며 노래를 부른다.
보아주고 들어주는 건 나 한 사람뿐인데
아이들은 우리 폭탄 대신 꽃을 손에 들자고,
세계를 향해 평화 시위를 하는 것만 같다.

FLOWERS INSTEAD OF BOMBS

The village of Srifa collapsed, became a wasteland, bombarded
by Israeli fighter-bombers. Rehearsing a play before the village festival,
many children died on the spot. Surviving girls come with discarded
artificial flowers, take me by the hand and ask me to take a picture.
Standing with the flowers at the place where their friends died they sing,
expressing the sorrows they have endured. I'm the only person watching
and listening; the children want to hold flowers instead of bombs
and stage a peaceful protest before the world.

Srifa, Lebanon, 2006.

전 사 의 딸

하늘만 뚫린 거대한 감옥 같은 팔레스타인 난민촌
'아인 알 할웨'의 아이들은 태어나면서부터
가난과 전쟁의 공포를 공기처럼 마시며 자란다.
소녀의 아빠는 급진 해방 조직의 대표였고
나와의 인터뷰 이후 총격전에서 숨을 거뒀다.
다음해 다시 만난 소녀는, 동생들을 키우고 차를 내오고
요리를 해주며 움직이는 정물처럼 내 곁을 맴돈다.
벽에 난 총탄 구멍은 그대로인데, 소녀만 '슬픈 성숙'이다.
아홉 살 소녀의 명랑한 말소리와 웃는 모습을
한 번이라도 볼 수 있었다면 가슴이 덜 아팠을 텐데.

A WARRIOR'S DAUGHTER

The children of Ain al-Halwe, a Palestinian refugee camp like a giant prison that only the sky penetrates, grow up breathing the fear of poverty and war like air from birth. This girl's father was a representative of a radical liberation organization and died in a gunfight soon after an interview with me. The girl I met the next year hovers around me like a moving still life, raises her siblings, brings tea, cooks for me. The bullet holes in the wall are the same, only the girl has reached 'sad maturity.' It would have been less painful for me to ever hear the nine-year-old girl's cheerful voice and see her smile.

'Ain Al-Hilweh' Palestine refugee camp, Saida, Lebanon, 2007.

페 샤 와 르 시 장 의 신 발 수 선 공

페샤와르 시장에서 신발을 수선하는 소년.
이 아이의 손을 거치면 불편했던 신발도
발에 딱 맞는다며 찾아오는 이들로 분주하다.
지난해부턴 직접 디자인한 신발도 출시했다.
귀중한 연장통에는 색 바랜 사진을 붙여놓았다.
"제게 기술을 물려주고 돌아가신 아빠인데요.
'얘야, 나보다 더 단단하고 멋진 신발을 만들렴.'
지금도 저를 보며 잔소리하는 것 같아요, 하하."
일은 사람을 강하게 만든다.
전심전력으로 일을 해나가고 책임지는 과정 속에서
기쁨을 맛보고 자기 절제로 단련된 아이의 인격은
훨씬 앞선 곳으로 뚜벅뚜벅 나아가고 있으니.

A SHOEMAKER AT PESHAWAR MARKET

A boy mending shoes at Peshawar market. It is bustling with people coming to
say that shoes that were uncomfortable, once they pass through this child's
hands, fit perfectly on their feet. He has also launched shoes he designed himself
from last year. A faded photograph was attached to his precious tool box.
"That's my father who passed on the craft to me before he passed away.
'Son, make shoes that are stronger and smarter than I do.' I have the impression
he's still nagging at me. Ha ha." Work makes people strong. The character of
the child who has experienced joy in the process of working wholeheartedly
and taking responsibility, trained by self-discipline, is moving far ahead.

Peshawar, Khyber Pakhtunkhwa, Pakistan, 2011.

흙 벽 돌 찍 는 아 이 들

파키스탄 어디서나 볼 수 있는 흙벽돌 공장.

이 붉은 벽돌은 색이 곱고 단단해 세계에 수출된다.

더는 밀려날 곳 없는 전쟁 난민과 극빈층이

마지막으로 내몰리는 일자리이기도 하다.

"5살 때부터 벽돌을 찍었어요. 하루 14시간씩요.

아빠가 다치고 빚을 져서 제가 집안을 책임져야 해요.

제 꿈은요, 학교요, 학교 다니는 거요.

책을 읽고 친구들이랑 노는 거요.

일어나서 어디로든 걷고 뛰는 거요."

오늘도 파키스탄에서만 약 170만 명의 아이들이

온종일 앉은걸음으로 흙벽돌을 찍고 있다.

CHILDREN MAKING BRICKS

Clay brick factories can be found everywhere in Pakistan. The red bricks
are exported to the world because of their fine color and hardness. It is also
the last job for the war refugees and the poorest, who have nowhere else to go.
"I have been making bricks since I was 5 years old. 14 hours a day. My dad
got hurt and is in debt, so I have to take care of the family. My dream? School,
to go to school. It's reading books and playing with friends, being able to
get up, go walking and running anywhere I want." Today, in Pakistan alone,
about 1.7 million children sit making clay bricks all day long.

Peshawar, Khyber Pakhtunkhwa, Pakistan, 2011.

IN THE DESERT AT SUNSET

After a long day, as the sun goes down, the boy driving
his sheep home is lost in thought. What is going on
inside that child right now? A child who seems to
have an intuition of the wonders of the abyss and
the mysteries of life, which suddenly come with cold and
heat, discomfort and hardship, despondency, loneliness,
and fear in the wild. No one can tell whether the light of
this moment, permeating like a long shadow, will come
back to life in 10 or 30 years, and become wings that will
soar again. Children need private time alone. They need
natural shade and darkness, solitude and deep thought.

Tell Beydar, Kurdistan, Syria, 2008.

노을 지는 사막에서

긴 하루가 지나고 태양이 기울자
양떼를 몰고 귀가하던 아이가 생각에 잠긴다.
지금 저 아이 안에 무슨 일이 일어나고 있는 걸까.
야생의 자연 속에서 추위와 더위, 불편과 고됨,
막막함과 외로움, 무서움과 함께 문득 찾아드는
심연의 경이와 생의 신비를 직감하는 듯한 아이.
긴 그림자처럼 스미던 이 순간의 빛이
10년 후, 30년 후, 어느 날 번쩍 되살아나
다시 솟구칠 날개가 되어줄지, 아무도 모른다.
아이에겐 홀로 있는 내밀한 시간이 필요하다.
자연스런 그늘과 어둠, 고독과 침잠이 필요하다.

봄 을 기 다 리 며

하늘과 땅이 하나인 듯 새하얀 설원의 쿠르디스탄.
폭설로 하루 일거리를 공친 구두닦이 아이들이
총성의 공포도 잊고 추위도 배고픔도 잊고
허리까지 쌓인 눈 속을 신나게 달린다.
눈 속에 싹트는 작은 새싹 하나라도 먼저 보고
언 강 아래로 흐르는 봄의 물소리를 먼저 듣고
종알종알 속삭이고 노래하며 봄을 찾아 나선다.
아이들은 봄이다. 그 자체로 봄이다.
설원에 어깨 걸고 선 쿠르드 아이들이
이 분쟁의 땅에서 간절히 평화의 봄을 부른다.

WAITING FOR SPRING

Kurdistan is a snowy field where the sky and the earth are one. Shoe-shine
children unable to get work in the heavy snow, forget the fear of gunshots,
forget the cold and hunger, and run cheerfully through snow piled up to
their waists. Seeing first at least one small sprout emerging from the snow,
hearing first the sound of spring water flowing down the frozen river,
whispering and singing, they set out in search of spring. Children are spring.
They are truly spring. Kurdish children, standing shoulder to shoulder in
the snow, earnestly call for a spring of peace in this land of conflict.

Van, Kurdistan, Turkiye, 2006.

어 린 양 을 안 고

하카리에 폭설이 내리면 총성마저 멈춘다.
눈이 강제한 짧고도 차가운 평화다.
쿠르드 해방을 위해 저기 자그로스 산맥으로 떠난
형과 누나들이 살아있는지 마음이 시린데
눈 속에 갇혔어도 어린 양은 태어난다.
"어린 양을 돌보는 건 저희들 몫이에요.
봄이 오면 양과 함께 산 높이 오를 거예요.
이 양이 자라 새끼를 낳고 또 새끼를 낳고 낳으면
누나랑 형들이 돌아올 날이 있겠죠, 그렇죠?"

HOLDING A LAMB

When snow falls in Hakkari, even the gunfire stops. It's a short, cold peace
imposed by the snow. Hearts yearn to know if older brothers and sisters, who left
for the Zagros Mountains to liberate the Kurds, are still alive, while lambs are
born even if they are locked in by snow. "It is our responsibility to take care of
the lambs. When spring comes, I will climb the mountain with the sheep.
When this lamb grows up and gives birth to a baby and to another baby,
there will be a day when our older sisters and brothers will come back, right?"

Hakkari, Kurdistan, Turkiye, 2006.

영원하라, 체 게바라

볼리비아의 오지 마을 '라 이게라'는
체 게바라가 최후를 맞이한 곳이다.
그는 헝클어진 머리칼로 피기침을 토하면서
두 눈을 뜬 채 이 외진 곳에서 총살당했다.
"진정한 혁명가를 이끄는 건 위대한 사랑의 감정이다."
쿠바 혁명의 권력과 영예를 뒤로 한 채
중남미 민중의 해방을 위해 볼리비아로 떠나
참혹하게 '실패한 혁명가'로 생을 마친 게바라.
그러나 그날 그의 심장을 관통했던 총성은
반세기가 지난 지금도 맑은 눈빛을 지닌
소년 소녀의 가슴을 관통하고 있으니.
매일 아침 들꽃을 꺾어다 놓아주는
이 마을 소녀가 가만히 고개를 숙인다.
"그라시아스 니냐." (고맙다 소녀야.)

FOREVER, CHE GUEVARA

La Higuera, a remote village in Bolivia, is the place where Che Guevara met his end. He was shot with his eyes open in this remote location as he coughed up blood through his messy hair. "It is a feeling of great love that drives true revolutionaries." Leaving behind the power and honor of the Cuban revolution, Guevara left for Bolivia for the liberation of the people of Latin America and ended his life as a wretched 'failed revolutionary.' But the gunshot that pierced his heart that day still pierces the hearts of boys and girls with clear eyes half a century later. This village girl who picks wild flowers every morning and lays them quietly bows her head. "Gracias, Niña." (Thank you, little girl.)

La Higuera, Santa Cruz, Bolivia, 2010.

파슈툰 소녀들

미국의 계속되는 침공과 산사태로 피폐해진
아프가니스탄 산악 국경 마을의 파슈툰 소녀들.
잘 웃지도 않고, 소리 내어 울지도 않고,
젖은 눈동자로만 지난 일들을 증언한다.
선생도 없는 학교에 모여 손 칠판 하나에
돌려가며 글자를 쓰다가 집으로 돌아가는 길.
영하의 추위에 난로도 외투도 양말도 없이
벌벌 떨던 소녀들이 묵연히 앞을 응시한다.
폭격과 가난, 그리고 여자의 몸을 뒤덮는
숙명으로부터 자유로운 저 먼 곳을 보는 것일까.
소녀들은 이 추운 꿈을 품에 꼬옥 안는다.

PASHTUN GIRLS

Pashtun girls in a mountain border village in Afghanistan, devastated
by continued American invasions and landslides. They don't laugh much,
they don't cry out loud, only their moist eyes testify to the past. On the way
home, after meeting at a school without a teacher and writing letters on
a blackboard by hand, the girls, who had been shivering in the freezing cold
without a stove, coat or socks, silently stare in front of them.
Are they looking at a faraway place free from bombing, poverty, and the fate
that covers a woman's body? The girls embrace this cold dream tightly.

Drosh, Khyber Pakhtunkhwa, Pakistan, 2011.

파슈툰 소년들

이 높고 험하고 외진 마을을 찾아온 나를
놀람과 경계, 슬픔으로 바라보던 파슈툰 소년들이
폭격에 죽은 가족과 친구들 사연을 얘기하다
어느새 어린 매의 눈동자가 되어가고 있었다.
그래, 그 눈빛이다.
알렉산더도 영국도 소련과 미국조차 물리치며
이 땅을 '제국의 무덤'으로 만든 파슈툰의 눈빛.
아이들아, 네 안에는 푸른 빛이 살아있으니.
부디 죽지 말고 다치지 말고 살아서 다시 만나자.

PASHTUN BOYS

When I came to this high, rugged and remote village, the Pashtun boys
looked at me with surprise, vigilance and sadness, then told stories about
their family and friends who died in the bombing. Suddenly, their eyes
became those of young hawks. Yes, those eyes, the eyes of Pashtun, who
defeated Alexander, Britain, the Soviet Union, and even the United States,
and made this land the "Graveyard of Empires." Children, bright light lives
within you. Please don't die, don't get hurt, live and let's meet again.

Drosh, Khyber Pakhtunkhwa, Pakistan, 2011.

RUN, CHILDREN

Even on a plain with no end in sight, children with a single deflated ball
do not notice the passing of time. The only thing that resonates in the plain
full of silence is the beating of strong hearts and the sound of laughter.
Children need the vastness of being. Not the excessive interest and
protection of parents and adults, but the open space of nature, freedom,
and the air of freedom. There, children take a deep breath and travel to
their own secret galaxy, make mistakes and worry on their own, find their
own way, have adventures with friends, cry, laugh and grow up. In the
midst of freedom and struggle, rebellion and challenge, failure and recovery,
the unique individuality that only that child is born with will awaken.

Tell Beydar, Kurdistan, Syria, 2008.

달려라 아이들아

끝이 보이지 않는 평원에서도 아이들은
바람 빠진 공 하나로 시간 가는 줄 모른다.
정적만이 가득한 평원에 울리는 건
강인한 심장의 고동소리와 웃음소리뿐.
아이들에겐 존재의 광활함이 필요하다.
부모와 어른들의 과잉된 관심과 보호가 아닌
대자연의 여백과 자유, 자유의 공기 말이다.
그 속에서 아이들은 깊은 숨을 쉬며
자신만의 비밀스런 은하를 여행하고
혼자서 저지르고 애태우고 스스로 헤쳐가고
친구와 모험하며 울고 웃고 자라갈 테니.
자유와 분투, 반항과 도전, 실패와 일어섬 속에
그 아이만이 타고난 고유한 개성이 깨어날 테니.

대추야자를 운반하며

오늘은 불타는 누비아 사막에서 혼신으로 키워낸
종려나무에서 달콤한 대추야자를 수확하는 날.
열 살 무함마드는 대추야자를 노새에 실어
강 건너로 운반하는 책임을 맡았다.
사막의 맹수들과 여러 위험으로부터 친구들과 함께
무사히 임무를 수행하겠다는 의지에 찬 얼굴이다.
수단 사막의 아이들은 잘 알고 있다.
자신만의 세계를 획득하고 자유를 넓혀가려면
공동의 책임과 의무를 다 해내야만 한다는 걸.
다시 만난 무함마드는 일주일에 걸친 임무를 마치고
앓아 누웠으나, 씨익 웃는 천진한 소년의 얼굴 위로
강인한 사내의 위엄이 서려 있었다.

CARRYING DATE PALMS

Today is the day to harvest sweet date palms from palm trees that
have been raised carefully with all their strength in the burning
Nubian desert. Ten-year-old Muhammad was given the responsibility of
transporting the dates across the river on mules. His face is full of determination
to carry out the mission with friends, safe from the wild beasts of the desert
and various dangers. The children of the Sudan desert know well that
in order to acquire our own world and expand our freedom, they must fulfill
our common responsibilities and obligations. When I met Muhammad again,
he was lying ill after the week-long mission, but the dignity of a strong man
loomed on the face of the innocent, grinning boy.

Old Dongola, Nubian, Sudan, 2008.

바 라 만 봐 도 좋 은 친 구

이슬람 최대 명절인 이드 알 아드하.
한 대지에서 한 식구로 살아온 소와 양에게
정성껏 꽃 장식을 해주고 기도를 바친 뒤,
신선한 고기를 세 개의 바구니에 나누어 담아
가족, 친지 그리고 가난한 이웃과 나눈다.
무엇보다 이 날은 아이들의 축제 날이다.
말린 꽃잎과 향료를 띄운 물에 몸을 씻고
선물 받은 옷을 입고 나와 기분이 들뜬 소녀들은
말 한마디에도 꺄르르 웃음을 터트린다.
어떤 이해관계도 없이 그냥 사람과 사람으로,
함께 있는 것만으로 좋은 그냥 친구인 친구로,
어린 날 순수한 우정을 다져가는 것.
이것이 인생에서 모든 관계의 기초가 된다.

GOOD FRIENDS, EVEN JUST LOOKING

Eid al-Adha is one of the biggest Islamic festivals. After giving flowers of
decoration with all their heat and offering prayers to cows and sheep who have
lived as part of the family on the same land, the fresh meat is divided into three
baskets and shared with family, friends and poor neighbors. Above all, this day
is a children's festival. After washing in water with dried petals and spices,
then emerging after putting on clothes received as gifts, the excited girls burst
out laughing at every word they say. Building pure friendships in childhood,
simply person to person without any selfish interest, as friends who are simply
good friends just by being together, that is the basis of all relationships in life.

Sargodha, Punjab, Pakistan, 2011.

불가촉천민 소년의 기도

열두 살 비벡은 불가촉천민 부부의 자식이다.
식당에서 허드렛일을 하면서도 매일 자기 손으로
빨아 다린 셔츠와 바지를 단정히 차려 입고 나선다.
꽃을 좋아하는 나를 알아보고 짜이를 내올 때면
찻잔 옆에 무심한 척 꽃송이를 놓아주는 아이.
비벡의 작은 방에는 몇 권의 책과 기도문이 있고
꽃향기 그윽한 흙마당에는 흰 빨래가 빛난다.
날 때부터 주어진 이 낡은 카스트의 천대와 차별 속에서
아름다움에 대한 감각, 총명한 일머리, 인간의 절도와 기품,
이런 품성을 갖기까지 그 고통과 눈물을 나는 안다.
비벡이 날마다 작은 성상에 물을 부으며 기도를 한다.
"저에게 인내를 주세요. 제가 용기 있게 자라면
어려운 이들에게 일용할 우유 같은 사람이 될게요.
저에게 지혜를 주세요. 제가 선생님이 되면
저 같은 아이들을 품어 줄 나무 같은 사람이 될게요."

THE UNTOUCHABLE BOY'S PRAYER

Twelve-year-old Vivek is the child of an Untouchable couple. While he does chores
in the restaurant, he goes out in a neat shirt and trousers that he washes and irons
by hand every day. He recognizes me as a flower-loving person and puts a flower next
to the teacup pretending to be indifferent when he brings me a cup of tea. There are
a few books and prayers in Vivek's small room, and white laundry shines in his
flower-scented dirt yard. I know the pain and tears of having such a character, a sense
of beauty, intelligent work, human moderation and dignity, amidst the contempt
and discrimination of this old caste system given from birth. Vivek pours water on
a small statue every day and prays. "Give me patience. If I grow up courageously, I will
become a person like daily milk for those in need. Give me wisdom. When I become
a teacher, I will become a person like a tree who will embrace children like me."

Patha Karka village, Uttar Pradesh, India, 2013.

둥글게 동네 한 바퀴

맨발의 아이가 폐타이어를 굴리며 골목길을 달린다.
세계 어느 마을에서나 아이들은 둥근 공, 둥근 구슬,
둥근 굴렁쇠만 있으면 앞으로 앞으로 달려 나간다.
그래, 아이야, 태양은 둥글고 지구는 둥글단다.
살아있는 것은 다 동그란 길을 돌아 나온단다.
오늘이 빛나지 않아도 구름 너머에 태양이 빛나고
이 길이 빛나지 않아도 어둠 속에서 별들이 빛나니.
내일은 둥근 것. 희망은 둥근 것. 사랑은 둥근 것.

ONCE ROUND THE NEIGHBORHOOD

A barefoot child runs down the alley, rolling a worn-out tire. In any village
in the world, children run ahead, all they need is a round ball, a round marble,
or a round hoop. Yes, child, the sun is round and the earth is round.
All living things run along a circular path. Even if today it is not shining,
the sun is shining beyond the clouds, and the stars shine in the darkness
even if this path is not bright. Tomorrow is round. Hope is round. Love is round.

Jatkara village, Madhya Pradesh, India, 2013.

CHILDREN ARE AMAZING

Young brothers holding trusting hands go walking
across the wilderness in a strong wind
to meet their mother, who has gone to work.

Ah, in the universe man is a thinking reed.*
Between the 'human misery' living a short and
painful life on a single planet, and the 'human greatness'
that yet loves, cares for, and thinks about others,
the children who have come to Earth are trembling starlight.

In this so dangerous world, in this age with
its uncertain future, children who open a new world,
bridging the gap between human misery and greatness,
children are amazing.

Children, who cry first, laugh first,
who are both weakest and strongest,
who find their own way and move ahead
without hesitation, children are amazing.

Children are the vanguard of the times.
Children are human hope.
Children are light in the darkness.

Dohak Baba Fakheer village, Punjab, Pakistan, 2011.

아이들은 놀라워라

어린 형제가 일 나간 엄마를 마중하러
거센 바람 부는 황야를 가로질러
믿음의 손을 붙잡고 나아간다.

아, 우주 가운데 인간은 생각하는 갈대이다.*
한 톨의 지구에서 짧고도 괴로운 생을 사는 '인간의 비참'
그럼에도 서로 사랑하고 헌신하고 사유하는 '인간의 위대'
그 사이에서, 지구에 온 아이들은 흔들리는 별빛이다.

이토록 위험 가득한 세계 속에서
이렇게 앞이 보이지 않는 시대 속에서
인간의 비참과 위대 사이를 가르며
새로운 세상을 열어가는 아이들은,
아이들은 놀라워라.

가장 먼저 울고 가장 먼저 웃고
가장 연약하고 가장 강인하고
자신들만의 길을 찾아서 거침없이
앞을 향해 나아가버리는 아이들은,
아이들은 놀라워라.

아이들은 시대의 전위여라.
아이들은 인간의 희망이어라.
아이들은 어둠 속 빛이어라.

* 파스칼에게서 일부 따옴(Adapted from Blaise Pascal)

전쟁의 레바논에서, 박노해. Park Nohae in the battlefield of Lebanon, 2007.

박노해

1957 전라남도에서 태어났다. 16세에 상경해 낮에는 노동자로 일하고 밤에는 선린상고(야간)를 다녔다. **1984** 27살에 첫 시집『노동의 새벽』을 펴냈다. 이 시집은 독재 정권의 금서 조치에도 100만 부 가까이 발간되며 한국 사회와 문단을 충격으로 뒤흔들었다. 감시를 피해 사용한 박노해라는 필명은 '박해받는 노동자 해방'이라는 뜻으로, 이때부터 '얼굴 없는 시인'으로 알려졌다. **1989** 〈남한사회주의노동자동맹〉(사노맹)을 결성했다. **1991** 7년여의 수배 끝에 안기부에 체포, 24일간의 고문 후 '반국가단체 수괴' 죄목으로 사형이 구형되고 무기징역에 처해졌다. **1993** 감옥 독방에서 두 번째 시집『참된 시작』을 펴냈다. **1997** 옥중에세이『사람만이 희망이다』를 펴냈다. **1998** 7년 6개월 만에 석방되었다. 이후 민주화운동 유공자로 복권됐으나 국가보상금을 거부했다. **2000** "과거를 팔아 오늘을 살지 않겠다"며 권력의 길을 뒤로 하고 비영리단체 〈나눔문화〉(www.nanum.com)를 설립했다. **2003** 이라크 전쟁터에 뛰어들면서, 전 세계 가난과 분쟁의 현장에서 평화활동을 이어왔다. **2010** 낡은 흑백 필름 카메라로 기록해온 사진을 모아 첫 사진전「라 광야」展과「나 거기에 그들처럼」展(세종문화회관)을 열었다. 12년 만의 시집『그러니 그대 사라지지 말아라』를 펴냈다. **2012** 나눔문화가 운영하는 〈라 카페 갤러리〉에서 상설 사진전을 개최, 21번의 전시 동안 35만 명의 관람객이 다녀갔다. **2014** 아시아 사진전「다른 길」展(세종문화회관) 개최와 함께『다른 길』을 펴냈다. **2019** 박노해 사진에세이 시리즈『하루』,『단순하게 단단하게 단아하게』,『길』,『내 작은 방』을 펴냈다. **2020** 첫 번째 시 그림책『푸른 빛의 소녀가』를 펴냈다. **2021**『걷는 독서』를 펴냈다. **2022** 12년 만의 시집『너의 하늘을 보아』를 펴냈다. 30여 년간 써온 한 권의 책, '우주에서의 인간의 길'을 담은 사상서를 집필 중이다. '적은 소유로 기품 있게' 살아가는 〈참사람의 숲〉을 꿈꾸며, 시인의 작은 정원에서 꽃과 나무를 심고 기르며 새로운 혁명의 길로 나아가고 있다.

매일, 사진과 글로 시작하는 하루 〈박노해의 걷는 독서〉 ⓘ park_nohae Ⓕ parknohae

Park Nohae

Park Nohae is a legendary poet, photographer and revolutionary. He was born in 1957. While working as a laborer in his 20s, he began to reflect and write poems on the sufferings of the laboring class. He then took the pseudonym Park Nohae ("No" means "laborers," "Hae" means "liberation"). At the age of twenty-seven, Park published his first collection of poems, titled *Dawn of Labor*, in 1984. Despite official bans, this collection sold nearly a million copies, and it shook Korean society with its shocking emotional power. Since then, he became an intensely symbolic figure of resistance, often called the "Faceless Poet." For several years the government authorities tried to arrest him in vain. He was finally arrested in 1991. After twenty-four days of investigation, with illegal torture, the death penalty was demanded for his radical ideology. He was finally sentenced to life imprisonment. After seven and a half years in prison, he was pardoned in 1998. Thereafter, he was reinstated as a contributor to the democratization movement, but he refused any state compensation. Park decided to leave the way for power, saying, "I will not live today by selling the past," and he established a nonprofit social movement organization "Nanum Munhwa," meaning "Culture of Sharing," (www.nanum.com) faced with the great challenges confronting global humanity. In 2003, right after the United States' invasion of Iraq, he flew to the field of war. Since then, he often visits countries that are suffering from war and poverty, such as Iraq, Palestine, Pakistan, Sudan, Tibet and Banda Aceh, in order to raise awareness about the situation through his photos and writings. He continues to hold photo exhibitions, and a total of 350,000 visitors have so far visited his exhibitions. He is writing a book of reflexions, the only such book he has written during the thirty years since prison, "The Human Path in Space." Dreaming of the Forest of True People, a life-community living "a graceful life with few possessions," the poet is still planting and growing flowers and trees in his small garden, advancing along the path toward a new revolution.

⟨Park Nohae's Reading while Walking Along⟩ ⓘ park_nohae ⨍ parknohae

저서   Books

박노해 사진에세이 시리즈

01 하루 02 단순하게 단단하게 단아하게
03 길 04 내 작은 방

박노해 시인이 20여 년 동안 지상의
멀고 높은 길을 걸으며 기록해온
'유랑노트'이자 길 찾는 이에게 띄우는
두꺼운 편지. 각 권마다 37점의 흑백
사진과 캡션이 담겼다. 인생이란 한 편의
이야기이며 '에세이'란 그 이야기를
남겨놓는 것이니. 삶의 화두와도 같은
주제로 해마다 새 시리즈가 출간된다.

136p ｜ 20,000KRW ｜ 2019-2022

Park Nohae Photo Essay

01 One Day 02 Simply, Firmly, Gracefully
03 The Path 04 My Dear Little Room

These are 'wandering notes' that
the poet Park Nohae has recorded
while walking along the Earth's long,
high roads for over twenty years,
a thick letter to those who seek for
a path. Each volume contains 37
black-and-white photos and captions.
Life is a story, and each of these
'essays' is designed to leave that story
behind. A new volume is published
every year like a topic of life.

너의 하늘을 보아

12년만의 신작 시집. 무언가 잘못된
세상에 절망할 때, 하루하루 내 영혼이
희미해져갈 때, 빛과 힘이 되어줄 301편의
시. 고난과 어둠 속에서도 '빛을 찾아가는
여정'에 자신을 두었던 박노해 시인의
투혼과 사랑의 삶이 전하는 울림. 그 시를
읽기 전의 나로 돌아갈 수 없는 강렬한
체험. "아무것도 없다고 생각되는 순간
조차, 우리에게는 자신만의 하늘이 있다."

528p ｜ 19,500KRW ｜ 2022

Seeing Your Heaven

A new collection of poems, the first in 12 years.
301 poems that will give you light and strength
when you despair in a world gone wrong,
when your soul seems to be fading away
day by day. The reverberations of the life of
love and fighting spirit of poet Park Nohae,
who set out on a 'journey in search of light'
in the midst of hardship and darkness.
An intense experience that makes it impossible
to return to who I was before I read the poems.
"Even when we think there is nothing,
we each have our own heaven."

걷는 독서

단 한 줄로도 충분하다! 한 권의 책이
응축된 듯한 423편의 문장들. 박노해
시인이 감옥 독방에 갇혀서도, 국경 너머
분쟁 현장에서도 멈추지 않은 일생의
의례이자 창조의 원천인 '걷는 독서'.
온몸으로 살고 사랑하고 저항해온 삶의
정수가 담긴 문장과 세계의 숨은 빛을
담은 컬러사진이 어우러져 언제 어디를
펼쳐봐도 지혜와 영감이 깃든다.

880p ｜ 23,000KRW ｜ 2021

Reading While Walking Along

One line is enough! 423 sentences, one whole
book condensed into each sentence. 'Reading
While Walking Along' is a lifelong ritual and
source of creation by Park Nohae who never
stopped, even after being confined in solitary
confinement in a prison cell or at the scene of
conflicts beyond the border. The aphorisms that
contain the essence of his life, in which he has
lived, loved and resisted with his whole body,
are harmonized with color photos that contain
the hidden light of the world, delivering wisdom
and inspiration wherever we open them.

푸른 빛의 소녀가

박노해 시인의 첫 번째 시 그림책. 저 먼 행성에서 찾아온 푸른 빛의 소녀와 지구별 시인의 가슴 시린 이야기. "지구에서 좋은 게 뭐죠?" 우주적 시야로 바라본 삶의 근본 물음과 아이들의 가슴에 푸른 빛의 상상력을 불어넣는 신비로운 여정이 펼쳐진다. "우리 모두는 별에서 온 아이들. 네 안에는 별이 빛나고 있어."(박노해)

72p l 19,500KRW l 2020

The Blue Light Girl

Poet Park Nohae's first Poetry Picture Book. The poignant tale of the Blue Light Girl visiting from a distant planet and a poet of Planet Earth. "What is good on Earth?" The fundamental question of life seen from a cosmic perspective. A mysterious journey inspiring an imagination of blue light in the heart of the children. "We are all children from the stars. Stars are shining in you."(Park Nohae)

다른 길

"우리 인생에는 각자가 진짜로 원하는 무언가가 있다. 분명, 나만의 다른 길이 있다." 인디아에서 파키스탄, 라오스, 버마, 인도네시아, 티베트까지 지도에도 없는 마을로 떠나는 여행. 그리고 그 길의 끝에서 진정한 나를 만나는 새로운 여행에세이. '이야기가 있는 사진'이 한 걸음 다른 길로 우리를 안내한다.

352p l 19,500KRW l 2014

Another Way

"In our lives, there is something which each of us really wants. For me, certainly, I have my own way, different from others"(Park Nohae). From India, Pakistan, Laos, Burma, Indonesia to Tibet, a journey to villages nowhere to be seen on the map. And a new essay of meeting true self at the end of the road. 'Image with a story' guide us to another way.

그러니 그대 사라지지 말아라

영혼을 뒤흔드는 시의 정수. 저항과 영성, 교육과 살림, 아름다움과 혁명 그리고 사랑까지 붉디 붉은 304편의 시가 담겼다. 인생의 갈림길에서 길을 잃고 헤매는 순간마다 어디를 펼쳐 읽어도 좋을 책. 입소문만으로 이 시집을 구입한 6만 명의 독자가 증명하는 감동. "그러니 그대 사라지지 말아라" 그 한 마디가 나를 다시 살게 한다.

560p l 18,000KRW l 2010

So You Must Not Disappear

The essence of soul-shaking poetry! This anthology of 304 poems as red as its book cover, narrating resistance, spirituality, education, living, the beautiful, revolution and love. Whenever you're lost at a crossroads of your life, it will guide you with any page of it moving you. The intensity of moving is evidenced by the 60,000 readers who have bought this book only through word-of-mouth. "So you must not disappear." This one phrase makes me live again.

노동의 새벽

1984년, 27살의 '얼굴 없는 시인'이 쓴 시집 한 권이 세상을 뒤흔들었다. 독재 정부의 금서 조치에도 100만 부 이상 발간되며 화인처럼 새겨진 불멸의 고전. 억압받는 천만 노동자의 영혼의 북소리로 울려퍼진 노래. "박노해는 역사이고 상징이며 신화다. 문학사적으로나 사회 사적으로 우리는 그런 존재를 다시 만날 수 없을지 모른다."(문학평론가 도징일)

172p l 12,000KRW l 2014
30th Anniversary Edition

Dawn of Labor

In 1984, an anthology of poems written by 27 years old 'faceless poet' shook Korean society. Recorded as a million seller despite the publication ban under military dictatorship, it became an immortal classic ingrained like a marking iron. It was a song echoing down with the throbbing pulses of ten million workers' souls. "Park Nohae is a history, a symbol, and a myth. All the way through the history of literature and society alike, we may never meet such a being again."(Doh Jeong-il, literary critic)

아이들은 놀라워라

박노해 사진에세이 05

초판 1쇄 발행 2022년 9월 30일

사진·글 박노해
번역 안선재
편집 김예슬, 윤지영
표지 디자인 홍동원
자문 이기명 아날로그 인화 유철수
제작 윤지혜 홍보 마케팅 이상훈
인쇄 자문 유화컴퍼니 인쇄 세현인쇄
제본 광성문화사 후가공 신화사금박

발행인 임소희
발행처 느린걸음
출판등록 2002년 3월 15일 제300-2009-109호
주소 서울시 종로구 사직로8길 34, 330호
전화 02-733-3773
팩스 02-734-1976
이메일 slow-walk@slow-walk.com
홈페이지 www.slow-walk.com
instagram.com/slow_walk_book

ⓒ 박노해 2022
ISBN 978-89-91418-34-9 04810
ISBN 978-89-91418-25-7 04810(세트)

번역자 안선재(안토니 수사)는 서강대학교 명예교수로
50권 이상의 한국 시와 소설의 영문 번역서를 펴냈다.

Children are Amazing

Park Nohae Photo Essay 05

First edition, first publishing, Sep. 30, 2022

Photographed and Written by Park Nohae
Translated by Brother Anthony of Taizé
Edited by Kim Yeseul, Yun Jiyoung
Cover Designed by Hong Dongwon
Consulted by Lee Ki-Myoung
Photographic Analogue Prints by Yu Chulsu
Print Making by Yun Jihye
Marketing by Lee Sanghoon
Print Consulted by UHWACOMPANY

Publisher Im Sohee
Publishing Company Slow Walking
Address Rm330, 34, Sajik-ro 8-gil, Jongno-gu,
Seoul, Republic of Korea
Tel 82-2-7333773 Fax 82-2-7341976
E-mail slow-walk@slow-walk.com
Website www.slow-walk.com
instagram.com/slow_walk_book

© Park Nohae 2022
ISBN 978-89-91418-34-9 04810
ISBN 978-89-91418-25-7 04810(SET)

Translator An Sonjae(Brother Anthony of Taizé)
is professor emeritus at Sogang University.
He has published over fifty volumes of
translations of Korean poetry and fiction.